Health Zone

Stay Clear!

What YOU Should KNOW about SKIN CARE

Sandy Donovan

illustrations by Jack Desrocher

Consultant Sonja Green, MD

Lerner Publications Company
Minneapolis

All characters in this book are fictional and are not based on actual persons. The characters' stories are not based on actual events. Any similarities thereof are purely coincidental.

Copyright © 2009 by Lerner Publishing Group, Inc.

Lerner Publications Company
A division of Lerner Publishing Group, Inc.
241 First Avenue North
Minneapolis, MN 55401 U.S.A.

Website address: www.lernerbooks.com

Library of Congress Cataloging-in-Publication Data

Donovan, Sandra, 1967.
    Stay clear!: What You Should Know about Skin Care / by Sandy Donovan ; illustrated by Jack Desrocher.
        p.   cm. — (Health zone)
    Includes bibliographical references and index.
    ISBN 978-0-8225-7550-4 (lib. bdg. : alk. paper)
    1. Skin-Care and hygiene—Juvenile literature. 2. Beauty, Personal—Juvenile literature. I. Desrocher, Jack, ill. II. Title.
    RL87.D64 2009
    646.7'26—dc22   2007043623

Manufactured in the United States of America
1 2 3 4 5 6 — BP — 14 13 12 11 10 09

Table of Contents

A Big fat ZIt

That's what Marco was staring at in the bathroom mirror. Or, rather, that's what was staring back at Marco. Two brown eyes. One small nose. One slightly crooked mouth. And one giant zit.

"Great," Marco muttered to himself. "Just what I need on the first day of sixth grade."

This was supposed to be one of the best days of Marco's life. He was leaving elementary school behind forever. He was finally joining the real world of middle school. He'd been looking forward to this day all summer.

Marco had everything ready. His favorite jeans and a cool new shirt were hanging in the closet. His backpack was stuffed with school supplies. He was ready to take on the world and make new friends. Maybe he'd even try out for the football team.

But now Marco had a problem. How could he make new friends with this volcano in the middle of his face? He glanced back into the mirror. *Was the zit actually growing?* He shouldn't have had that candy bar yesterday. That's what his mom always said: stay away from junk food. It didn't seem to matter what Marco ate, though. He always got zits at the worst possible time. And this one was the worst of them all.

"Leave it alone," Marco said to himself. He tried to distract himself by brushing his teeth. He knew he should keep his hands off the pimple. Picking at it would only make it worse. But it felt like a hot wasp's nest, right under his nose. It looked like a cranberry. Marco knew he shouldn't do what he was about to do. **He knew that it was the worst thing that he could do. *But he couldn't help himself.***

He squeezed.

Chapter 1

Skin: What's It All About?

Quick question:
What's something you can wear as a baby and never outgrow?

Answer: skin!

It still fits!

Think about it—a lifetime is a long time for skin to last.
But it does. Most of us take our skin for granted. We don't give it a thought until a problem like a pimple flares up. But our skin is a living part of us. It's the largest organ in our bodies. It's also one of the most important body parts. Sure, we need our lungs to breathe and our brains to think. But without skin, none of these other pieces would last long.

Skin covers us and keeps all our other parts sealed up inside us. Skin also protects our bodies. It helps keep them cool or warm. It gives us our sense of touch. Not bad for something as thin skinned as, um, skin.

Three Layers Deep

Skin might seem thin. But it is made up of three layers. The outer-most layer is actually dead skin cells. That's right! We're all walking around wearing nice protective coats of dead cells. Here's how it works.

The outer skin layer is called the epidermis.

At the bottom of the epidermis is the basal layer. New skin cells are always forming there. Once formed, these new cells start a journey up through the epidermis. The whole trip takes about two to eight weeks. As these newer cells rise up, they push older, dead cells to the surface. These old, dead cells are the ones that do the job of covering and protecting our bodies. But they don't stick around long. They're always flaking off. Then newer cells rise up to take their place. **In fact, you flake away about forty thousand dead skin cells** *each minute* **of the day!**

THAT'S A LOT OF DEAD WEIGHT! Each year, you probably "shed" about 9 pounds (4 kilograms) of dead skin cells.

What Are Your Blood Vessels?

Blood vessels are tiny tubes that help keep your body's cells healthy. Some vessels deliver oxygen and nutrients to cells. Others take waste and unwanted stuff away. Blood vessels are in the dermis. You may be able to spot some of them if you look closely. They look like thin blue lines. You may be able to see some on your hands or wrists. The epidermis there is often thin. If you can't see any on yourself, take a look at an older person's hands. Everybody's dermis gets thinner as they grow older.

The second layer of skin is the dermis.

The dermis is where your sense of touch is located. We feel things because sensory cells, located in the dermis, can sense pressure, heat, cold, and pain. The sensory cells pass these signals on to nerve endings. The nerve endings send the signals to the brain. Then the brain sends messages to the rest of the body. All of this message-sending takes place in the body's central nervous system. And it takes place so fast you don't even know it's happening. Ever notice how fast you move your hand away when it touches something hot like a stove? The instant your hand touches that hot item, the nerve endings in your dermis send an alert to the brain: **"Look out! Hot stuff!"** The brain responds by sending another message to your arm and hand muscles: **"Pull back! Too hot to touch!"**

This takes place so fast it might seem like you didn't even have time to recognize the hot feeling. Pretty amazing stuff.

Just What Is a Tattoo?

Tattoos are made from piercing the skin with an ink-filled needle. Tattoo artists are skilled at creating designs with these needles. Tattoos are permanent. That's because the ink is injected deep into the dermis. Safety is a big issue with tattoos. A tattoo can cause a skin infection if it's not applied correctly. An unclean needle can even spread serious diseases such as HIV, which leads to AIDS. Only trained professionals know how to properly apply tattoos.

Sending speedy alerts isn't the only amazing work the dermis does. It also makes oil and sweat. Sounds kind of gross, doesn't it? But the skin makes oil and sweat for good reasons. The oil (called sebum) has lots of jobs. It travels through oil glands (sebaceous glands) to the surface of the skin. There it mixes with dead skin cells to form a waterproof barrier. The barrier keeps your skin smooth and keeps water away from the rest of your body. It also keeps bacteria off your hair follicles (the tiny tubes where hair starts growing).

Everybody sweats. Even when you don't feel like you're sweating, you are. All day long, small amounts of sweat are traveling up through tiny holes called pores and onto your skin's surface. There, the sweat and sebum mix to form a film. The film protects the skin. And it stops too many of those dead cells from flaking away at once. It can also help you get a grip on something you want to pick up.

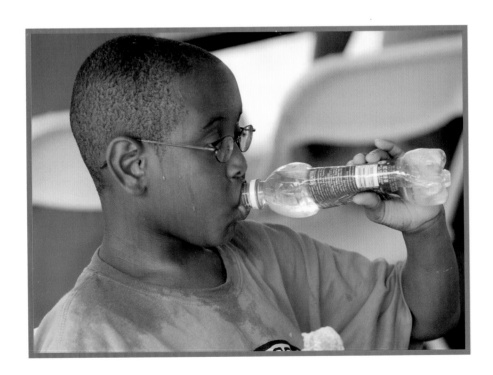

The third layer of skin is the subcutaneous layer.

This layer is made up of fat. The fat helps keep the rest of the body warm. It helps protect the body from bumps and falls too. It is also where hair follicles are located. Follicles continue on through the dermis and onto the skin's surface. They act like a guide for hair. In the dermis layer, every hair follicle meets up with a sebaceous gland. The sebaceous gland adds a drop of sebum to the hair as it grows. The sebum protects the hair. It also gives your hair its shine.

Keeping Your Cool
(and Your Heat)

Blood vessels, hair follicles, sweat and oil glands—there are a lot of body parts at work inside your skin. One of the things they work hardest at is keeping your body from getting too hot or too cold. The inside of your body needs to stay at about 98.6° F (37° C). Not an easy thing to do when you're out in the hot sun, cold snow, and all temperatures in between! But the parts that make up your skin really know how to jump to action when it comes to keeping your body temperature steady.

The sensory cells in the dermis do the first job. They figure out whether the outside temperature is too hot or too cold. They are constantly sending weather reports to the nerve endings. In turn, the nerves send them to a thermometer in the brain. When the brain begins to sense that things are getting too warm or too cold, it starts giving orders to the skin.

Sometimes the body starts to overheat. The blood vessels get word that it's time to start trying to unload extra heat. To do this, they bring the warmest blood closest to the body's surface. You may have noticed that your face gets red when you're hot. That's the warm blood traveling near the surface to try to cool down. At the same time, the sweat glands go into overdrive. They start making more and more sweat the hotter the body gets. The sweat travels to the skin's surface, bringing extra heat with it. As the air helps the sweat to evaporate (turn from liquid to vapor), the body cools down.

The brain reacts just as quickly when a cold front moves in. Blood vessels narrow to try to keep the warm blood safe from the cold outer elements. A tiny muscle called the erector pili pulls on your body hair to make it stand up. This reaction, called pilomotor reflex, is what makes **goose bumps** on your skin. The raised hairs help to trap a thin layer of air just above your skin. This helps keep your body warm.

Adding Color

Let's talk more about the epidermis. Everyone's outer layer of skin is made up of dead skin cells. But not everyone's skin looks the same. Skin seems to come in an endless number of colors and patterns. Some people have moles or birthmarks. Others might have freckles. Why?

Skin color comes from a substance called melanin. Melanin protects skin from the sun. The sun sends out ultraviolet (UV) rays. These rays can burn and damage skin. Melanin reflects or absorbs UV rays. This keeps the rays from burning the skin. The more melanin your body makes, the darker your skin color is.

Our genes—the traits we get from our parents—decide how much melanin we make. People whose ancestors lived in areas that got lots of sun (like central Africa or southern Asia) produce more melanin than those whose ancestors lived in places where the sun isn't as strong (like northern Europe). Fair-skinned people burn much faster than dark-skinned people because they don't have as much melanin to protect them. But some fair-skinned people have small spots where their skin actually makes a bunch of melanin. These small spots are freckles.

DID YOU KNOW?
About one in every ten people has one or more "café-au-lait" (coffee with milk) marks. These oval spots on the skin are where extra melanin produces what looks like a coffee stain.

People whose skin makes lots of melanin may not burn as quickly as fair-skinned people. But that doesn't mean that their skin is safe from the sun. Melanin doesn't give you perfect protection from UV rays. Get too much sun and your skin can get damaged. It doesn't matter how dark your skin is to begin with. Too much sun exposure can cause skin cancer. Skin cancer is becoming more common as more people sunbathe. Experts figure that about one out of every five people in the United States will get skin cancer in their lifetime. Most skin cancers can be treated. **But like all cancers, skin cancer can be fatal.**

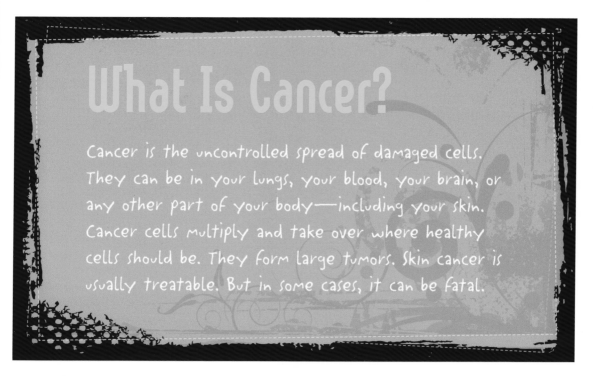

What Is Cancer?

Cancer is the uncontrolled spread of damaged cells. They can be in your lungs, your blood, your brain, or any other part of your body—including your skin. Cancer cells multiply and take over where healthy cells should be. They form large tumors. Skin cancer is usually treatable. But in some cases, it can be fatal.

Chapter 2

IS YOUR Skin GETTING A LIFE OF ITS OWN?

Remember when
you never gave your skin a second thought?

You've had it your whole life, but for the most part, it's just hung around on your body.
Sure, you might have had a couple of bad sunburns. And you might have wished your skin was darker, lighter, or maybe had fewer freckles. But it probably hasn't been a huge area of concern.

And then all of a sudden—right in your preteens and early teens—skin seems to become an issue. Pimples are popping up on your face. You might start to see lines on your back, hips, thighs, and chest. (These are called stretch marks. More about them later.) What's going on? What's causing all these changes? **And most important, *how can you stop them from wrecking your life?***

Blemishes, Pimples, and Zits

No matter what you call them, you probably don't want to see these trouble spots cropping up on your face. Unfortunately, the prime time for pimples to begin is right around the preteen years. *Why does this happen?*

Remember those hair follicles and oil glands that live in your dermis? The sebum produced by the oil glands travels through the follicles to the skin's surface. It provides moisture and protection to the skin. It gives your hair its shine. At least, that's what's supposed to happen.

Sometimes, however, things don't go so smoothly. Sometimes the sebum doesn't make it to the skin's surface. Instead, it gets stopped by the hair growing from the follicle. This causes a jam inside the follicle. As more sebum is produced, it builds up behind the jam. This "trapped" oil allows bacteria to grow inside the follicle. It's this bacteria that causes trouble. The bacteria soon cause an inflammation. And can you guess what an inflammation on your skin looks like? Hint: the **four signs** of inflammation are **swelling, redness, heat,** and **pain.** Sound familiar? *Yep, that's a pimple.*

So why do pimples tend to form during the preteen years?
Well, it's all because of chemicals called hormones. Young adults' bodies produce a lot of a hormone called androgen.

Androgen causes follicles to get bigger. And it causes them to produce more sebum. This makes it more likely that the follicle will get blocked and turn into a pimple. And you may have noticed that most pimples show up on your face, neck, back, chest, and shoulders. That's because these areas have the most hair follicles. The more follicles you have in an area, the more likely it is that some of them will get jammed up.

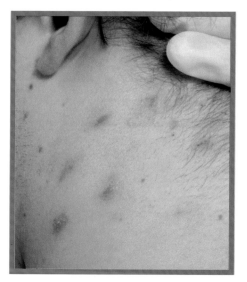

Just What Is Puberty?

Puberty is the time when your body and mind begin to develop and change from childhood to adolescence. It usually begins sometime between ages eight and fifteen. During puberty, your body will grow quickly. The only time in your life when you grow faster is when you're a baby. During puberty, you will go through lots of changes. These changes will have many effects on your skin and the rest of your body.

All teens and preteens get pimples from time to time. But not all pimples are created equal. Let's take a look at the two main types.

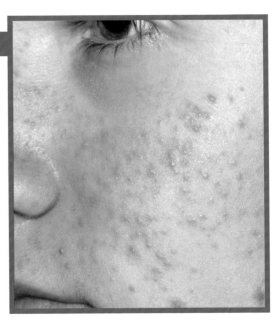

Whiteheads

Sometimes a pimple stays beneath the skin. When this happens, you see a small white bump on the skin. That's called a whitehead.

Blackheads

Other times, a pimple opens up onto the skin's surface. As the sebum mixes with the outside air, it turns black. That's called a **blackhead**.

Often whiteheads or **blackheads** become inflamed right at the skin's surface. This causes pink- or red-colored pimples. If these pimples get infected, they may become filled with white- or yellow-colored pus. *Acne* is the term used to describe an outbreak of blackheads or whiteheads.

YOU'RE NOT ALONE. About 80 percent of people between the ages of eleven and thirty have acne outbreaks at some point.

What's Your Skin Type?

Skin comes in all shades and sizes. But most people's skin falls into one of four categories.

Dry skin may get flaky. It can crack easily. It will feel and look better if you use lotion to keep it moisturized. Also avoid superhot water when washing.

Normal skin isn't too dry or greasy. It tends not to be too sensitive to most products.

Oily skin sometimes looks greasy, or oily. People with oily skin may be at a higher risk for acne.

Combination skin has some oily areas and some normal to dry areas. The more oily areas are usually the forehead, nose, and chin. These areas are often referred to as the T-zone.

Check out the activity at the back of this book to find out which type of skin you have!

Acne

So now you know what acne is. *But why do some people get it while others don't?* It's all a matter of science. It's called genetics. It has to do with genes passed down from parents to kids. So if your birth parents had acne as preteens, chances are that you will too.

Does this mean that if your parents had acne, you're doomed? Maybe or maybe not. The causes of acne are mostly out of your control. But there are some things you can do to keep it under control. Check out chapter 4 to learn more.

Stretch Marks

Pimples aren't the only skin issue that crops up during the preteen and teenage years. **Stretch marks are also common.** These lines often form on the back, hips, thighs, and chest. They may look like the beginning of a rash.

Stretch marks form when a person grows or gains weight. When the body gets bigger, the skin needs to keep up. Skin usually does an amazing job at keeping up with your body. But during puberty, skin might get overstretched. When this happens, it has trouble producing enough collagen. (Collagen is a material that builds connecting tissues in skin.) Without enough collagen, tiny scars may form. It's these scars that show up as lines on the skin. Any time your body is growing quickly, stretch marks might show up.

Puberty is one of the most common times for stretch marks to appear. But younger or older kids can get stretch marks too. Stretch marks may be red or purplish. The lines may seem to have a different texture than the surrounding skin. Most stretch marks from puberty tend to fade in time. Still, you may be more concerned with how they look now than with how they'll look in ten years. Check out chapter 4 for tips on dealing with stretch marks.

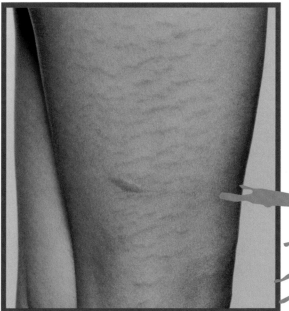

DID YOU KNOW?
Many bodybuilders get stretch marks when they gain muscles and rapidly change the shape of their body.

What's That Itch?

Rashes are another common skin problem. They can sting and itch. They can also be embarrassing, especially on the face, arms, or hands. Some kids may even tease kids who have rashes or other skin conditions. But most rashes aren't contagious. Most rashes can be treated with medicines you can buy at the store. But it's always best to get a doctor's advice if you think you might have a skin condition. It's also important to remember that rashes are not the fault of the person who has them. They're no reason to make fun of someone. Whether you have had a skin condition or not, it's important to understand what they are. Then you won't be tempted to make anyone else feel bad because of a skin condition.

One common skin condition is eczema. Skin with eczema is itchy. It often has redness or swelling. It can even have blistering and scabbing. Eczema often affects only small patches of skin. It may come and go. Lots of people have patches of eczema when they are babies or toddlers. But most people grow out of it before they begin school. Most kids outgrow it by the time they are eighteen.

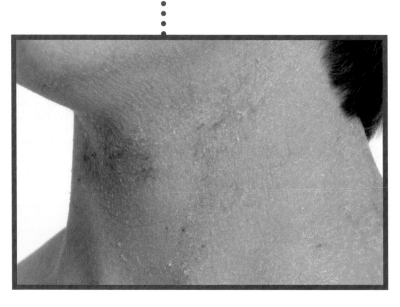

Cold Sores

Cold sores are clusters of small blisters. They usually form on the lips or around the mouth. They may be painful, but they're mostly harmless. They're caused by a virus. Once the virus strikes, the blisters form. They often break open and leak a clear fluid. After a few days, they usually turn into a scab. The scab may hang around for seven to ten days.

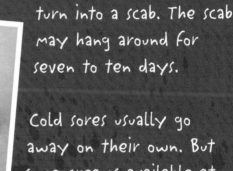

Cold sores usually go away on their own. But some creams available at drugstores may speed up the process. Cold sores are contagious. Wash your hands often if you have a cold sore or are around someone who does. Don't share water bottles, soda cans, or cups with someone who has one. And be sure not to share lip balm or lipstick. They can pass the infection from one mouth to another.

Psoriasis is another skin rash. It's not as common as eczema. But its impact can be severe. Psoriasis can cause patches of dry, red skin. It also can cause large areas of dry, silvery white, scaly skin. It's caused when new skin cells are produced anywhere from two to seven times as fast as normal. The older, dead cells do not flake off. Instead, they stick together and form silvery white scales. Kids who have psoriasis have a tough time dealing with the rash. But remember that it's not their fault. And it can't be spread from one person to another.

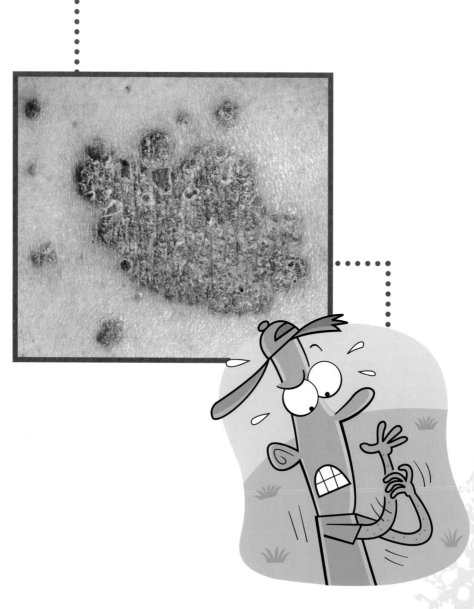

Some rashes are due to allergies. Allergies are caused by the immune system. The immune system fights off germs that make you sick. But some people have very active immune systems. These people's immune systems might react to dust, trees and flowers, or certain foods. The immune system's reaction makes these people feel ill. Their noses might run. Their eyes might feel scratchy. Or they might get rashes.

People can get red bumps called hives when they are allergic to foods such as nuts or fish. People can also get hives when they are allergic to medicines or insect bites. Hives can be itchy and uncomfortable. But they can't spread from one person to another. Hives can be serious, though. Sometimes they're the start of a more serious allergic reaction. If you have hives and your throat starts to itch or your stomach begins to feel funny, call a doctor right away. If your throat starts to swell or you feel short of breath, call 911.

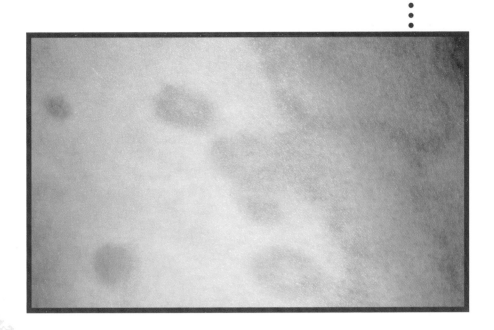

Chapter 3

TAKE GOOD CARE OF YOUR Skin

Skin is a major part of your body,

and it's got a lot in common with all of your other body parts

(think bones, muscles, heart, and brain).

All of these body basics are complex, living things that work together as part of one amazing system. And all the pieces of this system need to be cared for as part of a whole. *So, the most important things you do to take care of your whole body will take care of your skin as well.*

Getting enough sleep is a biggie. Bodies that are between ten and thirteen years old need around nine to ten hours of sleep a night. It's easy to find excuses not to get enough sleep. But if you want healthy skin, getting enough sleep is a must. Skin uses this downtime to repair itself from the stresses of the day. While the rest of the body is sleeping, skin cells are at work adding lost moisture. When bodies don't get enough sleep, the skin's appearance is often one of the most telltale signs. This is especially noticeable just under the eyes, where people's skin is about half as thin as skin on the rest of the face. The small lines, dark circles, or puffy areas that show up there are a sign that the skin needs more sleep time to repair itself.

Healthy foods are another simple ingredient for good skin. Just like the rest of the body, skin needs a balanced diet to be healthy. It needs protein for cells to grow and repair, carbohydrates for immediate energy, fats for stored energy, and vitamins and minerals for overall functioning. That's why it's important to eat a balanced diet with foods from all six food groups (fruits, vegetables, grains, meats and beans, milk, and oils). But, although some magazines may say that certain kinds of food will change or improve your skin, that's not really the case. It's true that some vitamins do have specific effects on the skin. For instance, vitamin A helps keep skin smooth and elastic. And vitamin B helps give skin its glossy finish. But almost everybody gets enough of these vitamins from a healthy diet, so taking extra vitamins or using skin-care products with these vitamins is not necessary, according to most skin doctors.

Clean Skin Essentials

All day long, our skin is exposed to dirt, oil, lotion, makeup, and other things that can smother it. But one of the best things about skin is that it's easy to keep clean. All you need is a daily wash of soap and water, in most cases. To set up a skin-cleaning routine for yourself, think about the different areas of your skin and what they go through in a typical day.

Most of your body is probably covered in clothes for most of the day and doesn't actually get too dirty. But some areas of your body produce odors throughout that day. Those areas are under your arms, in your pubic region, and on your feet. **To keep your whole body smelling sweet, you just need to shower or bathe once a day.** Adjust the water temperature so it feels warm, but not hot—hot water can dry out your skin and make you feel itchy and uncomfortable all day. Use a gentle soap, and focus on those areas that are actually dirty or smelly. Make sure you rinse all of your body with plenty of warm water—but there's no need to stay in a bath or shower longer than a few minutes— even if the water is just a little too warm, it can dry out your skin. Once you're finished, try to dry off by patting your towel all over you instead of rubbing it back and forth across your body. If you tend to have dry skin, then follow your bath or shower with some moisturizer right away.

Oh So Dry

Lots of things can cause excessively dry skin. Some people are born with very dry skin (African American skin tends to be dry), and some people live in environments that cause dry skin. For instance, being in extremely cold or windy weather can be drying to skin. Other causes of dry skin can be living in an arid (dry) climate, being exposed to a lot of indoor heating or air-conditioning, swimming in pools with lots of chlorine, or taking very hot showers. To minimize dry skin, try a cooler shower followed right away by all-over moisturizer. Also, put a layer of moisturizer on your face before you go out in the sun, wind, or cold and before diving into a chlorine-filled pool. And don't forget to rinse chlorine off your body as soon as possible.

African Americans and others with darker skin—that is, more melanin in the skin—can have more sensitive skin. Use extra caution when trying new products like moisturizer and makeup. Test them out on a small patch of skin first.

Be a Smart Shopper

Have you ever spent time in the skin-care aisle at a drugstore? Then you know there are hundreds of products available to clean your skin. Keeping track of all the ingredients can feel impossible. Many manufacturers claim that their products will make big changes to your skin. But with product prices ranging anywhere from one to one hundred dollars, it's important to know what you really need in a skin cleanser. Here are the basic types of skin soaps:

"Regular" Soaps

These are the most basic kinds of soaps, the ones that usually come in plain white bars. They are usually the least expensive soaps at the store, and they are very good at washing away dirt and oil from your skin. Their main ingredients are usually animal and vegetable fats. But regular soaps can be drying, especially when used on the face. If you have oily skin, regular soap may be perfect for you. If you have dryer skin, you may want to use these soaps only on odor-producing parts of your body like under your arms.

Common brand: Ivory

Soapless Soaps

These are soaps that have been developed to be less harsh than regular soaps. But instead of being made from animal or vegetable fats, like regular soaps, they are made from petroleum oils and other substances. Since they are gentler on the skin, many skin doctors recommend them for people with normal, sensitive, dry, or slightly dry skin.

Common brand: Lowila

Deodorant Soaps

These are soaps that have extra ingredients added to fight the bacteria that cause odors on skin. But those extra ingredients are not usually necessary to fight skin odors, and they can irritate dry skin. Most skin doctors recommend that you use these soaps only if you tend to sweat a lot. Try not to use them on your face, especially if you have dry skin.

Common brand: Dial

Moisturizing Soaps

These are soaps that have moisturizer added to them. Common added moisturizers are lanolin, mineral oil, cocoa butter, or olive oil. These soaps are gentler on skin than regular soaps, but they may feel like they leave a thin layer of grease on your skin. They are best for people with dry skin all over.
Common brand: Dove

Transparent Soaps

These soaps often look like orange-colored glass (they're not completely see-through, but they do have a clear appearance). Like moisturizing soap, they have added moisturizers, but they also have added glycerin or alcohol. These ingredients give them their clear look, but they can also cause them to be drying. They are best for people with sensitive but oily skin.
Common brand: Neutrogena

Lotion Soaps

These cleansers are mostly lotion with added soap. They have more moisturizer than moisturizing soaps. They come in pump dispensers and tend to be more expensive than bar or moisturizing soaps. They are best for dry or sensitive skin.
Common brand: Cetaphil

Clean Pits

The skin in your armpits begins to produce more sweat during puberty. Sweat is a healthy way for our skins to push out dirt, toxins, and other unwanted elements. But since armpits are an easy place for moisture like sweat to get trapped, it's also an easy place for body odors to grow. Keep your armpits fresh by washing them daily with soap. If needed, you can also start using a deodorant in the morning. If you start noticing wet marks or stains on your shirts, you may also want to try an antiperspirant deodorant. Antiperspirants help reduce the amount of sweat your glands produce.

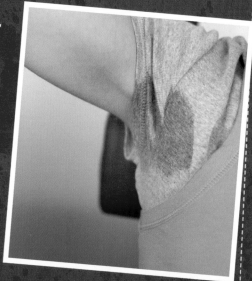

***Your face is home to the most delicate skin on
your body, so be extra gentle when washing it.***
It is thinner than the rest of your skin, so it doesn't need to be
scrubbed. You don't need fancy face soap. Just use a gentle soap
and warm—not hot—water. Make sure you rinse well with plenty
of warm water to remove all traces of soap. To dry, take a towel
and gently pat your face—rubbing back and forth with a towel
will bother gentle face skin even more than it irritates the skin on
the rest of your body. If the skin on your face gets dry and flaky,
add face moisturizer right after washing to keep it smooth.

What's That Really Mean?

You'll notice lots of big words on the containers of soaps and other skin-care products. Here's what some of the more common terms mean:

Non-comedogenic means it is free of oil or other ingredients known to clog pores. Non-comedogenic soaps, lotions, and makeup are key for keeping oily skin clear.

than just gentle cleansing for even the most sensitive skin. Every time you cleanse, its non-soap formula adds back moisture so skin retains resiliency and suppleness. Rich and non-irritating, it leaves skin more moisturized – without a filmy residue that can clog pores.
- Dermatologist recommended • Fragrance-free
- Non-comedogenic • Hypo-allergenic

Directions: Wet face and hands with lukewarm water.

Hypoallergenic means it is free of ingredients that can be irritating to skin. Using hypoallergenic products is a must for sensitive skin.

Play It Safe in the Sun

Protecting your skin from the harmful effects of the sun is probably the single best thing you can do for it. Unfortunately, that can be easier said than done. Playing in the sun and sunbathing are popular summer pastimes, and lots of people think that tanned skin looks good. But doctors agree that there is no such thing as a safe tan. In fact, tans and sun exposure are signs of sun damage, and although many people still think they look good for a few days, they cause big problems later. Skin that has been repeatedly exposed to the sun develops brown spots, wrinkles, and possibly even skin cancer as it grows older. That's a big price to pay for a short-lived suntan. Skin that's been in the sun a lot also ages much faster than skin that's been protected. Luckily, it can be pretty easy to keep your skin young and healthy.

DID YOU KNOW?
five or more sunburns double your risk of developing skin cancer.

Be SPF Savvy

You've probably seen SPF numbers on sunscreen bottles and tubes, but do you know what they mean? They are actually pretty simple to understand. An SPF number is a sun protection factor, and it tells you how much longer you can stay in the sun without burning when you apply that product. For instance, a sunscreen with an SPF of 15 means you can stay in the sun without burning your skin for fifteen times as long as you could without the sunscreen. So if your skin would normally burn in 20 minutes, when you coat your skin with SPF 15, you can stay in the sun for 5 hours (20 minutes times 15) without burning. All you really need to remember about SPF is that the higher the number, the longer you can stay in the sun. If you have fair or sensitive skin, you should wear an SPF of 30 or higher. If you have skin that rarely burns or is naturally brown or black, you can wear an SPF of 8 to 15.

The sun does its damage through powerful, invisible ultraviolet rays. So the trick to healthy skin is to keep those rays off of your skin. **One of the best ways to do this is** • • • **to keep skin covered up.** Try loose-fitting clothing and a wide-brimmed hat when you're going to be in the sun for a long time. Of course, sometimes you'll want to be in less clothing or even a swimsuit. **That's when you need to make sure to keep yourself under a layer** • • • **of sunscreen.**

Sunscreen reflects UV rays and keeps them from damaging your skin. Remember to apply sunscreen about twenty minutes before you go outside—that will give it time to soak into your skin and work better. Also, don't overlook areas like your ears, inner arms, the areas next to bathing suit straps and leg and arm openings, neck, hair part, and back (ask someone to help you get your whole back). Use a lip balm with an SPF of at least 15 on your lips. If you're going to be outside for a long time, bring your sunscreen and reapply every couple of hours.

Still Want a Tan?

Even when you know the facts about how dangerous sun can be to our skin, it can be hard to face a summer without a tan. Luckily, sunless tanning products let you enjoy the benefits of bronzed skin without the damage. Sunless tanners are lotions or sprays that contain an ingredient that reacts with your outer dead skin cells. It turns them brown. Sunless tanners are available at drugstores and grocery stores. And they work quickly: you can rub one into your skin in the morning and have a rich tan by the afternoon. Almost all available sunless tanners use the same active ingredients, so you don't need to buy the more expensive ones. Just remember to follow the directions carefully—and especially remember to wash your hands after applying (if you don't, you may end up with extra-tan palms). Try a sunless tanner first on an area of skin that others won't see, and if you like the results, repeat wherever you want a tan. One of the benefits of a sunless tan is that it's not permanent. It wears off naturally as your dead skin cells flake away, usually within a week.

Chapter 4

WHAT TO DO WHEN Trouble Strikes

The skin protects all other body parts.

It acts a bit like a shield.

So it makes sense that it often suffers from injuries. Skin can get rashes, infections, and cuts. Luckily, skin can recover from most of these problems. But sometimes, skin can use some help to repair itself. A general rule of thumb is that cuts longer than one-half inch (12 millimeters) usually need stitches. Cuts on the face most likely need stitches if they're longer than one-quarter inch (6 mm).

You can usually treat small cuts and scrapes at home. *(But be sure to show your injury to an adult to make sure it's not more serious than you think.)* The first step is to rinse the cut with cold, running water for several minutes. The water cleans the cut. Using cold water also causes your blood vessels to close up and slow the bleeding. Next, use a clean cloth to apply pressure to the cut for five to ten minutes. Then wash the cut gently with soap and water for five minutes. This helps make sure you get out any dirt that may be trapped in the cut. Finally, apply a bandage to the cut. You can use either a regular bandage or a liquid bandage. Liquid bandages are a clear substance that you brush onto the cut. Ask your parent or guardian which kind of bandage you should use. *If your cut or scrape doesn't get better within ten days or starts to become more red and swollen, call a doctor. It may be infected.*

What's That Scab?

You've probably formed hundreds of scabs in your lifetime. But what are scabs? They are just part of the body's natural healing process—sort of nature's own bandage. (Once you've got a scab, you don't need a bandage anymore). When skin gets cut, blood usually rushes to the surface. When this blood mixes with other cells, it forms a scab. And underneath that protective shell, the injured cells begin quickly producing new healthy cells. It's best not to pick at scabs. They're there for a reason. They protect the newly formed cells underneath until they're ready to take over on top of the skin.

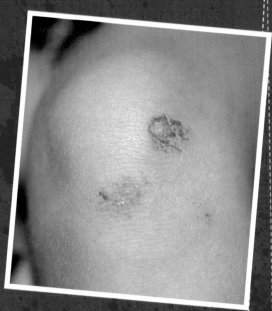

Dealing with Pimples

Perhaps it seems like you have a new zit every time you look in the mirror. Or maybe you just get an occasional pimple. Either way, dealing with pimples is never fun. One thing to remember is that you are not alone. Nearly every boy and girl in your school will have to battle pimples at some point.

Unfortunately, there's no simple cure-all for pimples or acne. You can't avoid flare-ups altogether. But don't give up the fight! A list of strategies for dealing with zits is below.

Keep your skin clean.

Wash your face once or twice daily with a mild cleanser and warm water. Don't use water that's too hot. And don't wash more than twice a day or scrub too hard. All of those actions can lead to irritation.

Keep your hands off.

Whatever you do, don't pick at pimples. Picking at them will make them more noticeable in the short run. It can also spread bacteria around your face and cause more breakouts. Hair products and hair's natural oils can also clog pores. So if you have long hair, it's a good idea to keep it off your face as much as you can.

DID YOU KNOW?
Scientists can make artificial skin using human skin cells and other materials. This real-looking skin can be used to cover serious burns or other skin injuries.

Untrue!

Don't believe these common acne myths.

The more you wash, the clearer your face will be. In fact, extra scrubbing can lead to extra dry or irritated skin—and more pimples.

Eating too much junk food causes zits. Of course, junk food is not good for any part of your body. But it does not cause breakouts.

The sun can help "dry up" acne. In reality, sun damage can lead to more pimples. It thickens the outer layer of skin and damages your pores. This leads to more blocked follicles and more zits.

Try a little medicine. Acne medication can't cure or prevent all breakouts. But it can keep them under control. It can even decrease the number of future breakouts. If you have oily skin, look for an astringent. Astringents contain ingredients for drying up oil. Try patting some on after you wash your face or even throughout the day. But look out for signs of dryness. If your skin is becoming too dry, stop using the astringent.

Another solution to dry up oily skin is to blot it with a tissue.
Most people who have pimples do not necessarily have oily skin on their entire face. Blotting your face can help remove oil from oily spots without leaving the rest of your skin feeling dry. To treat only problem areas, you might try a pimple cream with benzoyl peroxide. You can dry out affected areas by dabbing them with the cream. This will speed up the recovery process by helping to flake off dead skin.

See a doctor if you need to. If it seems impossible to control pimples with drugstore medicines, talk to your doctor.
No treatment is guaranteed to prevent pimples. But some prescription medicines and creams can help.

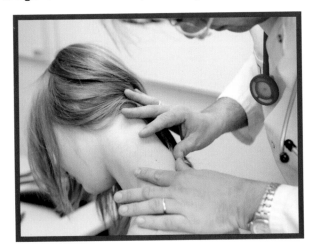

Tip: Don't ever wear makeup to bed (this goes for boys too!). It can clog pores and lead to pimples.

What's That REALLY Mean?

Ingredient lists on lotions and makeup can be long and complex. It can be hard to know what every ingredient is. And when you have oily or acne-prone skin, some of these ingredients can actually cause breakouts. Here's a list of ingredients that you should avoid if you have acne:

Acetylated lanolin alcohol
Cocoa butter
Heavy mineral oil
Isopropyl esters
Isopropyl myristate
Lanolin
Lanolin fatty acid
Linseed oil
Oleic acid
Olive oil
Petrolatum
Stearic acid

Dealing with Stretch Marks

Like pimples, stretch marks are often just a sign of puberty. And just as there's no cure-all for pimples, there's no easy way to avoid stretch marks. That doesn't mean you're helpless in dealing with them, though. See below for some tips on battling stretch marks.

Try a little makeup or sunless tanner.

Stretch marks are visible because they don't match the color of the rest of the skin. But a little makeup or sunless tanner can disguise the marks. It can make them blend in with the rest of the skin. Makeup can be a good camouflage. And a sunless tanner's ingredients can change the color of both the stretch marks and the surrounding skin. This will help the marks blend in. But beware: tanning will increase, not decrease, the appearance of stretch marks. This is because the marks themselves are a kind of scar. Sun damage will just make the scar more permanent. If you want stretch marks to fade, keep them covered with sunscreen.

Dress for success.

Stretch marks can be most annoying in the summer when you're wearing a bathing suit. But with a little clever clothing selection, you can cover up many stretch marks and still look cool. Girls can try boy-short bathing suits or tankinis. Boys can try longer board-short bottoms and tank tops.

Live with 'em.

If you do have stretch marks, take comfort in the fact that they're signs of healthy growing. Most people have them at some point in their lives. And they'll probably fade over time. Don't bother with creams and lotions that claim to get rid of stretch marks. They won't work. It's best to just accept them as a natural part of growing.

So now you know.

You're stuck with the skin you've got for the rest of your life. It's your job to take care of it and keep it healthy. Keep it clean, and don't dry it out. Protect it from the sun's rays.

If you get pimples, don't worry. It's a part of growing up. It happens to just about everybody at some time.

Just remember:
take good care of your skin,
and it will take good care of you.

Quiz

Now that you've read all about skin care, try this fun quiz to see how much you know. Please record your answers on a separate sheet of paper. (Answers appear at the bottom of page 57.)

1. **It's time for a day at the beach. You're ready for a day of fun. When should you put on your sunscreen?**

   a. about twenty minutes before you go outside

   b. the minute you get to the beach

   c. just as soon as you start to turn pink

2. **It's summer and your freckles are out in full force. What are these things?**

   a. signs of skin cancer

   b. spots where your skin produces super-powerful melanin

   c. blackheads

3. **What falls off of your skin each minute?**

   a. about 40,000 drops of sweat

   b. about 40,000 dead skin cells

   c. about 40,000 dead hairs

4. **A huge pimple has erupted in the middle of your face. What should you do?**

   a. squeeze it as hard as you can to get all the "stuff" out

   b. use a product with benzoyl peroxide and then keep your hands off it

   c. lay out in the sun for a couple hours to "dry it up"

5. Which of the following causes acne?

   a. too much homework

   b. using too much sunscreen

   c. plugged hair follicles

6. Which of the following isn't one of the main categories of skin type?

   a. combination skin

   b. oily skin

   c. perfect skin

7. What's one of the best ways to keep your skin healthy?

   a. get plenty of sun

   b. get plenty of rest

   c. use only expensive lotions

8. Something stinks, and it's you! Which of these areas is the least likely to be sweaty and smelly?

   a. your hands

   b. your feet

   c. under your arms

9. To get a tattoo or not to get a tattoo—that is the question. What's the biggest health-related drawback to getting one?

   a. You might not like it in five years.

   b. Your boyfriend or girlfriend might not like it.

   c. You might get a skin infection.

10. Stretch marks are caused by:

   a. overstretching of the skin

   b. an overactive immune system

   c. doing lots of stretching exercises

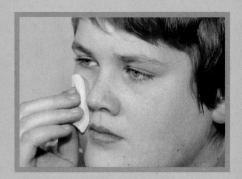

Take the Skin Test

What is your skin type? Try this simple test to find out if you have oily, dry, or combination skin.

What you'll need:

Washcloth

Soap

Clock

Small square of tissue paper

What you do:

Using the soap and washcloth, wash your entire face. Then pat it dry.

Wait 20 minutes. In the meantime, tear the tissue paper into ten small (penny-sized) pieces.

After you have waited 20 minutes, press pieces of tissue paper on different spots around your face. Spread them out all over your face.

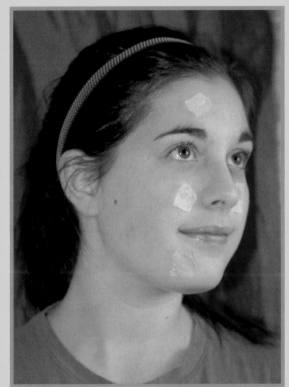

If the paper sticks to your skin, you have oily skin.

If the paper doesn't stick to you face, your skin is dry.

If the paper sticks only in certain spots— especially around your forehead, nose, and chin—you have combination skin.

Glossary

acne: an outbreak of blackheads or whiteheads

allergies: an overreaction of the immune system, the body system that fights off disease. The immune system of an allergic person may react to dust, trees and flowers, or certain foods.

bacteria: tiny living things that can't be seen with the eye but that can cause swelling, irritation, or infection

contagious: something that can be passed from one person to another

dermis: the second layer of skin. The dermis is where your sense of touch is located.

epidermis: the outer layer of skin

erector pili: a tiny muscle that can pull on body hair to make it stand up

follicle: a tiny tube in the skin where a hair begins to grow

hormone: a chemical produced by the body to direct and run a certain bodily function

sebum: an oily substance produced in the middle layer of the skin. Sebum mixes with dead skin cells to form a waterproof barrier that keeps your skin smooth and keeps bacteria off your hair follicles

subcutaneous: the deepest layer of skin. The subcutaneous layer is made up of fat.

toxin: a substance that collects in the body and causes it harm

The American Academy of Dermatology. "2007 Skin Cancer
Fact Sheet." *AAD*. N.d. http://www.aad.org/media/background/
factsheets/fact_skincancer.html (January 28, 2008)

Frankel, David H. *Field Guide to Clinical Dermatology*.
Philadelphia: Lippincott Williams & Wilkins, 2006.

National Institute of Arthritis and Musculoskeletal and Skin
Diseases. "Acne." *NIAMS*. N.d. http://www.niams.nih.gov/
Health_Info/Acne/default.asp (November 8, 2007).

Nemours Foundation. *KidsHealth*. 2007. http://www.kidshealth.
org/parent/ (November 8, 2007).

Novick, Nelson Lee, M.D. *Skin Care for Teens*. New York: Clarkson
N. Potter, 2000.

Novick, Nelson Lee, M.D. *Super Skin*. New York: Clarkson N.
Potter, 1988.

Papadopoulos, Linda. *Understanding Skin Problems: Acne,
Eczema, Psoriasis and Related Conditions*. West Sussex, UK:
John Wiley & Sons, 2003.

Sutton, Amy L. *Dermatological Disorders Sourcebook: Basic
Consumer Health Information about Conditions and Disorders
Affecting the Skin, Hair, and Nails*. Health Reference series.
Detroit: Omnigraphics Publishing, 2003.

Learn More about Skin Care

Brynie, Faith Hickman. *101 Questions about Your Skin That Got Under Your Skin ... Until Now*. Minneapolis: Lerner Publications Company, 2000. This book uses a question-and-answer format to discuss the structure, functions, diseases, and care of skin. It includes questions about hair, nails, aging, the effects of sun exposure, cancer, tattooing, and face-lifts.

Ceaser, Jennifer. *Everything You Need to Know about Acne: A Helping Book for Teens*. New York: Rosen Publishing, 2002. Ceaser dives into the science behind acne. She covers causes of the condition and discusses the drawbacks and benefits of different types of acne treatment.

Crump, Marguerite. *Don't Sweat It!: Every Body's Answers to Questions You Don't Want to Ask*. Minneapolis: Free Spirit Pub., 2002. Read more about acne, body odor, and other physical changes that happen during puberty.

Gregson, Susan R. *Skin Care*. Mankato, MN: LifeMatters, 2000. The author covers skin care for teens, focusing on two of the most common problems—acne and sun damage.

KidsHealth for Kids
http://kidshealth.org/kid
This site provides doctor-approved health information for kids. Use the site's search box to look up any skin-related topics.

Sheen, Barbara. *Acne*. San Diego: Lucent Books, 2004. This book focuses on acne, its causes, and its treatments. The author also includes a section on living with acne.

TeenHealthFX: Frequently Asked Questions and Answers about Skin Issues
http://www.teenhealthfx.com/answers/Health/subcategory.php?subsection=23
Use this site to browse through a long list of actual questions from teens. It covers topics including acne, stretch marks, boils, and other skin conditions.

York-Goldman, Dianne. *You Glow Girl! The Ultimate Health & Skin Care Guide for Teens*. New York: Quality Medical Publishing, 1999. This book gives practical tips for keeping your skin healthy and glowing—and helping to build your self-confidence in the process.

Photo/Illustration Acknowledgments

The images in this book are used with the permission of: © Phanie/ Photo Researchers, Inc., p. 4; © David Young-Wolff/Photographer's Choice/Getty Images, p. 6; © Sara Zinelli/Alamy, p. 9 (left); © age fotostock/SuperStock, pp. 9 (right), 19; © Luc Beziat/Taxi/Getty Images, p. 10; © Juncal/Alamy, p. 11; © Enigma/Alamy, p. 12; © Bubbles Photolibrary/Alamy, p. 13; © Ebby May/The Image Bank/Getty Images, p. 15; © Brand X Pictures, p. 16; © White Packert/The Image Bank/Getty Images, p. 17; © Dan Atkin/Alamy, p. 18; © Medical-on-Line/Alamy, pp. 21, 25; © Dr P. Marazzi/Photo Researchers, Inc., pp. 22, 29; © Mediscan/Visuals Unlimited, p. 26; © Oscar Burriel/Photo Researchers, Inc., p. 27; © Dr. Ken Greer/Visuals Unlimited, p. 28; © Clarissa Leahy/ Stone/Getty Images, p. 30; © George Doyle/Stockbyte/Getty Images, p. 32; © Stockbyte/Getty Images, p. 33; © iStockphoto.com/Jonathan Maddock, background on pp. 37, 38; ©Todd Strand/Independent Picture Service, pp. 37 (all), 38 (all), 41; © Stock4B/Getty Images, p. 39; © Sven Schrader/Taxi/Getty Images, p. 40; © Sally and Richard Greenhill/Alamy, p. 42; © Jeff Greenberg/Alamy, p. 43; © Profimedia International s.r.o./ Alamy, p. 46; ©Tae Photography/First Light/Getty Images, p. 48; © SCF/ Visuals Unlimited, p. 49; © G. Baden/zefa/CORBIS, p. 50; © Estelle Rancurel/Taxi/Getty Images, p. 51; © SGO/Image Point FR/CORBIS, p. 52 (top); © iStockphoto.com, p. 52 (bottom); © Ryuichi Sato/Taxi Japan/ Getty Images, p. 53; © Photodisc/Getty Images, p. 56; © iStockphoto.com/ Aman Khan , p. 57 (top); © iStockphoto.com/Anita Patterson, p. 57 (bottom); © Julie Caruso, pp. 58, 59.

Cover: © Jose Luis Pelaez, Inc./CORBIS.

About the Author

Sandy Donovan has written many books for young readers including *Billy Graham* (Biography, 2007) and *Protecting America* (How Government Works, 2004). She lives in Minneapolis with her family, Eric, Henry, and Gus.